D1187497

Illustrated by JORDI SOLANO

JUDY YOUNG

HU WAN
and the
SLEEPING DRAGON

Many centuries ago

One lived in the Forbidden City. At nine years of age his father died, leaving him the emperor of China.

The other was a nine-year-old peasant boy named Hu Wan.

there were two boys.

As Hu Wan worked in the garden beside his grandfather, he could just barely see the tallest roof in the Forbidden City standing gold against the sky.

"Is it true, Grandfather, that the City is filled with beautiful jewels?" Hu Wan asked.

"I have heard it is so," Grandfather answered, "but our eyes will never see them. No one is allowed to enter the City unless invited by the emperor. But do not forget, you have beautiful treasures, too."

Hu Wan knew Grandfather was talking about the colorful treasures hiding below the rich, dark soil. Orange carrots as bright as garnets, yellow onions as brilliant as gold, and purple beets, whose juice was ruby red. Pushing to rise above the soil were more treasures. Ivory cauliflower hid behind emerald leaves and broccoli grew like clusters of jade.

And then, there were the gourds. They were not good to eat but they would be made into ladles and bowls to be sold at the village market. Hu Wan looked at their twisty vines and smiled. He and his grandfather shared a secret about the gourds.

Each spring, when the gourds were just developing on the vine, Grandfather put a strangely shaped clay vessel around one special gourd. That gourd grew inside the vessel and in the fall when they cracked open the hardened clay, the gourd would be the same unusual shape. Once dried, Grandfather would scratch a design into the skin of the gourd and make it into a beautiful cricket cage. This spring, Grandfather gave Hu Wan the honor of shaping the vessel.

Throughout the summer when Hu Wan gently separated the leaves, his clay vessel lay in the tangle of vines surrounded by other gourds. Each day, he carefully checked the vessel, making sure no moisture had gotten into it.

One night, a huge storm brought heavy rains.

"The garden is flooding," Grandfather told Hu Wan.
"We must make frames out of sticks to keep the
gourds above the soggy ground or they will rot."

"You stay inside, Grandfather," Hu Wan said.
"I can do that."

"No," Grandfather insisted. "It will take both of us to
make sure the gourds are well protected."

The gourds did not suffer from the damp, but Grandfather did.
A chill took him and, with his face bright with fever, he lay cold
and shivering on the sleeping mat Hu Wan placed near the fire.

For five days it rained. Each day, Hu Wan checked the gourds.
And each day, he made soup for Grandfather from the garden's
vegetables.

The sun finally came out, but Hu Wan continued to tend the garden alone. It was many days before Grandfather weakly sat up and called to Hu Wan.

"There was a harvest moon last night," Grandfather said. "It's time to check the gourds."

As the sun turned dewdrops into a treasure of diamonds on the garden's leaves, Hu Wan thumped each of the gourds. Their hollow sound told him they were ripe and he cut them from the vines. Then, without breaking the clay vessel, he cut that gourd's stem as well.

Inside, Hu Wan ceremoniously placed the clay-covered gourd in front of his grandfather. But Grandfather did not pick it up.

"With the honor of shaping the gourd comes the honor of opening it," Grandfather said.

Hu Wan smiled, picked up the vessel, and brought it down onto the floor. The clay cracked and an oddly shaped gourd lay exposed among the pieces.

"It's beautiful," Hu Wan said, picking it up. There wasn't a blemish on it.

"What does it look like to you?" Grandfather asked.

Hu Wan knew this was an important question. It would determine how it would be designed.

"I think it looks like a sleeping dragon," he said, "with its tail wrapped around him."

"Yes, it does," Grandfather agreed. "But first, it must dry. Turn it every morning until the seeds rattle inside."

One morning, when Hu Wan turned the special gourd, he heard a rattle. Grandfather heard it, too. Grandfather took a small tool made of bone carved to a sharp point. He handed it to Hu Wan.

"Me?" Hu Wan asked in surprise.

"My hands are still shaky from my illness," Grandfather said. "And it's time for you to learn."

Hu Wan took the tool. He was so nervous the tool slipped and slashed the side of the gourd.

"Oh no!" he exclaimed.

"Don't worry," Grandfather said. "Mistakes can be turned into masterpieces. Look at it again."

Hu Wan looked at the gourd. "The slash looks like a closed eye," he said excitedly. He picked up the tool again.

Hu Wan carefully scratched into the gourd. Then he rubbed ink into the scratches. Soon, an image appeared of a sleeping dragon. He cut a circle from the top to make a lid, and poked many breathing holes through it.

Hu Wan looked at the finished cricket cage and frowned.

"It's not very good," he said, handing it to his grandfather. "Not like the ones you've made."

"Did you try your hardest?" Grandfather asked, turning the gourd in his hands.

"Yes," said Hu Wan.

"Then there is no need to feel bad," Grandfather said. "It is your first one. Skill comes only with practice."

Summer came to an end and autumn began turning the garden leaves from emeralds to ambers. One evening, Hu Wan sat in the garden and listened. It was good luck to hear the first cricket of fall. And better luck to catch it.

Hu Wan heard a chirp, and then another. Quickly, he reached under a leaf and grabbed a cricket. Taking it indoors, he lifted the lid on the sleeping dragon and dropped the cricket inside. All evening, the cricket chirped. Its sound echoed musically through the dragon's tail.

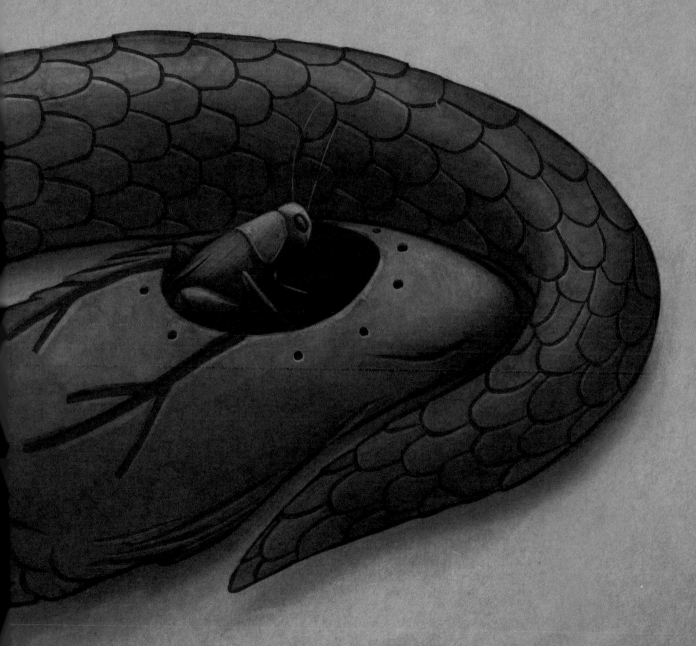

"Your gourd's shape made the cricket's song beautiful," Grandfather praised. Hu Wan smiled, hoping the cricket would also bring happiness and good luck.

The next day, Hu Wan carried a basketful of
ladles and bowls to sell at the village market.
A man dressed in an imperial uniform stood in
the middle of the marketplace.

"The young emperor has been saddened by the
death of his father," the man read from a scroll.
"We are seeking gifts to cheer him."

Hu Wan thought about the young emperor
all day. He knew how sad he would be if
illness had taken Grandfather.

That night, as Hu Wan lay on his sleeping mat,
the cricket started singing from inside the sleeping
dragon. Its beautiful song filled the darkness and
Hu Wan knew what he must do.

When the sun rose, Hu Wan took the sleeping dragon and walked toward the Forbidden City. When he reached the outer gates, a guard stopped him.

"I have a gift," Hu Wan stated, holding up the sleeping dragon.

The guard laughed at the crudely carved dragon. He pointed to tables where dozens of exquisite gifts had been left for the young emperor. There were animals carved from jade, game boards inlaid with jewels, and cricket cages made from ivory. Embarrassed by his humble offering, Hu Wan reluctantly placed the sleeping dragon among the beautiful gifts.

The next morning, Hu Wan and Grandfather worked in the garden, getting it ready before the snows covered the earth with sparkling crystals. Suddenly, the guard from the Forbidden City entered behind them, holding the sleeping dragon.

"Are you the one who gave this to the emperor?" the guard asked.

"Yes," Hu Wan said, hanging his head. "I'm sorry. I knew it was not worthy of His Majesty."

"There is no need for shame," the guard said. "The young emperor said a cricket singing from a dragon-shaped cage gave him sweet dreams."

"My cricket cage?" Hu Wan asked in amazement.

"Yes," said the guard, "and the emperor wants more carved gourds. You will be well paid."

All winter, as the earth slept, Hu Wan
thought about the lonely boy being cheered
by a cricket chirping in a sleeping dragon.

Spring and summer passed. When harvest season came again, Hu Wan stood in the garden and looked at the tallest roof of the Forbidden City. Then he carried a basket filled with many clay-covered gourds inside. Taking one, Hu Wan cracked it open and offered a strangely shaped gourd to his grandfather.

"I have been honored by the many treasures you have given me," Hu Wan said, bowing. "The honor of carving gourds for the emperor belongs to you, Grandfather."

Author's Note

For centuries, Chinese people have captured crickets, keeping them in small cages for the enjoyment of their song. The idea for *Hu Wan and the Sleeping Dragon* came after seeing a display of ancient cricket cages at the Nelson-Atkins Museum of Art in Kansas City, Missouri. Some were made of ivory but I was fascinated with ones made from gourds. There were other small items for crickets, too: little beds, tiny water dishes, feeding troughs, and delicate tongs used to pick up the crickets. The items on display were intricately carved and would have been possessions of a wealthy person, possibly an emperor. But, I imagined a peasant boy who would also enjoy the song of a cricket.

There are over nine hundred species of crickets. Most are nocturnal and spend their days hiding in grasses or under leaves, rocks, or fallen logs. Some species can fly, others can't, but most rely on their strong hind legs to jump away from predators.

After hatching from eggs, young crickets look like adult crickets but are smaller and don't have wings yet. Their wings develop as they grow over the summer. As fall approaches, adult male crickets make loud chirping sounds by rubbing their front wings together. A fun fact: if you count the number of chirps one cricket makes in 15 seconds and add 37, you will know approximately what the temperature is.

Hu Wan and the Sleeping Dragon is set in Beijing, China, where the world's largest ancient palace is located. Surrounded by walls that are 26 feet tall and 28 feet thick, and a moat 20 feet deep and 171 feet across, the Forbidden City has 9,999 rooms in 980 buildings. Twenty-four emperors have lived there, including Wanli, who in 1572 became emperor at nine years of age after the death of his father.

For Amelia Pendleton. Thanks for taking me to see the cricket cages!
—Judy

To all who have taught me what I needed to get here. To all who will teach me the rest.
—Jordi

Text Copyright © 2018 Judy Young • Illustration Copyright © 2018 Jordi Solano • All rights reserved. No part of this book may be reproduced in any manner without the express written consent of the publisher, except in the case of brief excerpts in critical reviews and articles. All inquiries should be addressed to: **Sleeping Bear Press**™ • 2395 South Huron Parkway, Suite 200, Ann Arbor, MI 48104 • www.sleepingbearpress.com • © Sleeping Bear Press • Printed in the United States • 10 9 8 7 6 5 4 3 2 1 • Library of Congress Cataloging-in-Publication Data • Names: Young, Judy, 1956- author. • Solano, Jordi, illustrator. • Title: Hu Wan and the sleeping dragon / written by Judy Young ; illustrated by Jordi Solano. • Description: Ann Arbor, MI : Sleeping Bear Press, [2017] • Summary: In 1572 Beijing, when a nine-year-old boy is named Emperor of China, Hu Wan offers the gift of a cricket cage carved from a gourd he and his grandfather grew. • Identifiers: LCCN 2017002859 • ISBN 9781585369775 (hard cover) • Subjects: • CYAC: Farm life–China–Fiction. • Grandfathers–Fiction. • Gourds–Fiction. • Crickets as pets–Fiction. • Kings, queens, rulers, etc.–Fiction. • China–History–Ming dynasty, 1368-1644–Fiction. • Classification: LCC PZ7.Y8664 Hu 2017 | DDC [E]–dc23 • LC record available at https://lccn.loc.gov/2017002859